HAROLD'S IMAGINATION

3 Adventures with the Purple Crayon

Afterword photo credits:
"An Off Day" courtesy of Philip Nel.
Crockett at seventeen photograph reproduced courtesy of the Queens Borough Public Library, Long Island
History Division, Frederick J. Webber Photographs.
Crockett with *Barnaby*, photographer unknown, courtesy of the Smithsonian Institution.
The Carrot Seed copyright Crockett Johnson, courtesy of HarperCollins Publishers.
Photo of Crockett Johnson and Ruth Krauss by Frank Gerratana. Image courtesy of the
Smithsonian Institution.
Original cover drawing for Harold and the Purple Crayon courtesy of the Smithsonian Institution.
David Johnson Leisk and his mother, Mary, photo courtesy of the Smithsonian Institution.
Nina Wallace photo by Agnes Goodman courtesy of Nina Landau Stagakis.
Harold Frank photo courtesy of Harold Frank.
Artist Crockett Johnson as drawn by Harold courtesy of the Smithsonian Institution.
Letters from Ursula Nordstrom and Ann Powers copyright HarperCollins Publishers.
New York Herald Tribune's Children's Spring Book Festival poster courtesy of Chris Ware.
Chinese, Hebrew, and German editions of *Harold* courtesy of Philip Nel.
Photo of Crockett Johnson in 1972 by Jackie Curtis.

ISBN 978-0-06-283945-9

Typography by Celeste Knudsen
18 19 20 21 22 SCP 10 9 8 7 6 5 4 3 2 1

First Edition

HAROLD'S IMAGINATION

3 Adventures with the Purple Crayon

Crockett Johnson

WITH AN AFTERWORD BY PHILIP NEL

HARPER
An Imprint of HarperCollinsPublishers

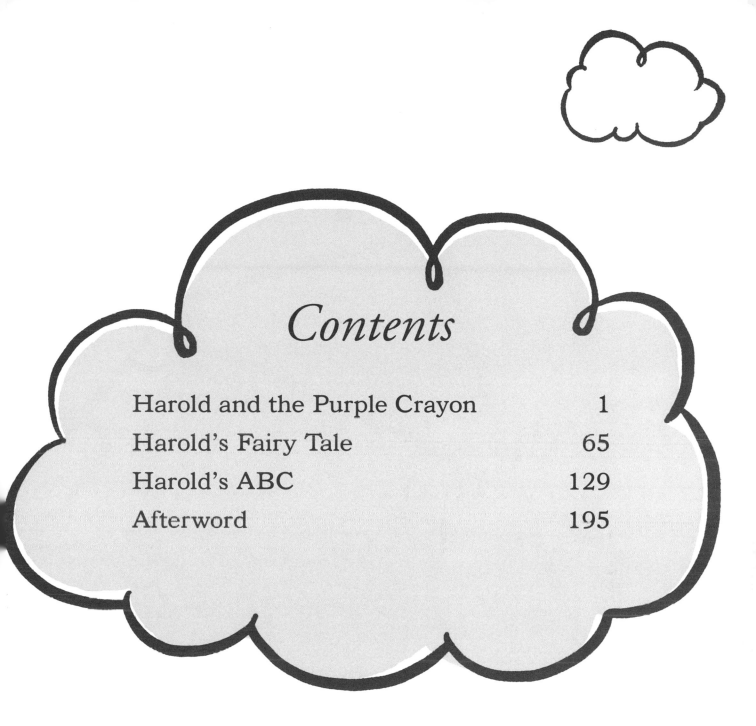

Contents

HAROLD

and the

PURPLE CRAYON

One evening, after thinking it over for some time, Harold decided to go for a walk in the moonlight.

There wasn't any moon, and Harold needed a
moon for a walk in the moonlight.

And he needed something to walk on.

He made a long straight path so he wouldn't get lost.

And he set off on his walk, taking his big
purple crayon with him.

But he didn't seem to be getting anywhere
on the long straight path.

So he left the path for a short cut across
a field. And the moon went with him.

The short cut led right to where Harold
thought a forest ought to be.

He didn't want to get lost in the woods.
So he made a very small forest, with just
one tree in it.

It turned out to be an apple tree.

The apples would be very tasty, Harold
thought, when they got red.

So he put a frightening dragon under the
tree to guard the apples.

It was a terribly frightening dragon.

It even frightened Harold. He backed away.

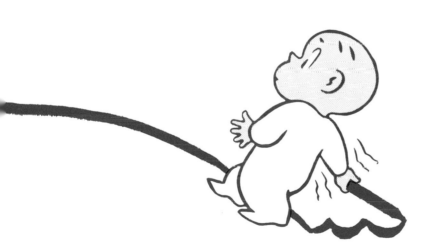

His hand holding the purple crayon shook.

Suddenly he realized what was happening.

But by then Harold was over his head in
an ocean.

He came up thinking fast.

And in no time he was climbing aboard a
trim little boat.

He quickly set sail.

And the moon sailed along with him.

After he had sailed long enough, Harold
made land without much trouble.

He stepped ashore on the beach, wondering
where he was.

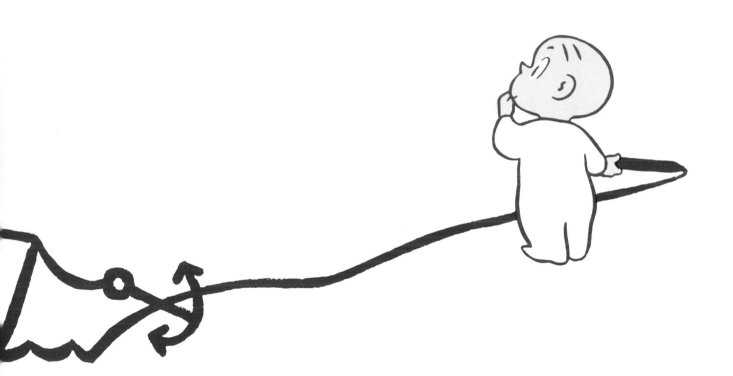

The sandy beach reminded Harold of picnics.

And the thought of picnics made him hungry.

So he laid out a nice simple picnic lunch.

There was nothing but pie.

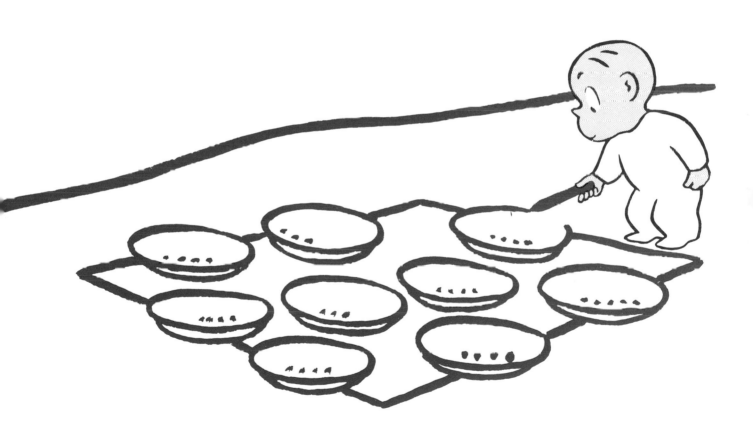

But there were all nine kinds of pie that
Harold liked best.

When Harold finished his picnic there was
quite a lot left.

He hated to see so much delicious pie go
to waste.

So Harold left a very hungry moose and a
deserving porcupine to finish it up.

And, off he went, looking for a hill to
climb, to see where he was.

Harold knew that the higher up he went,
the farther he could see. So he decided
to make the hill into a mountain.

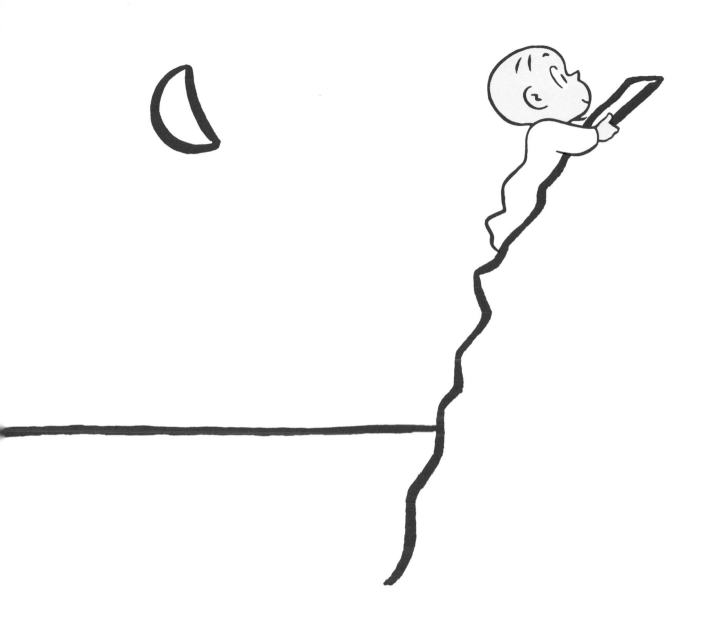

If he went high enough, he thought, he
could see the window of his bedroom.

He was tired and he felt he ought to be getting to bed.

He hoped he could see his bedroom window
from the top of the mountain.

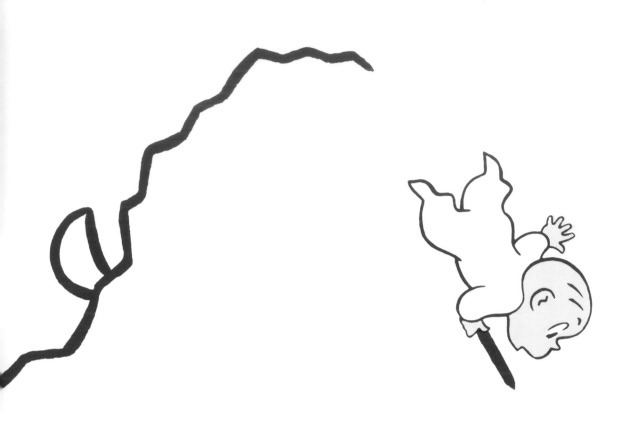

But as he looked down over the other side
he slipped—

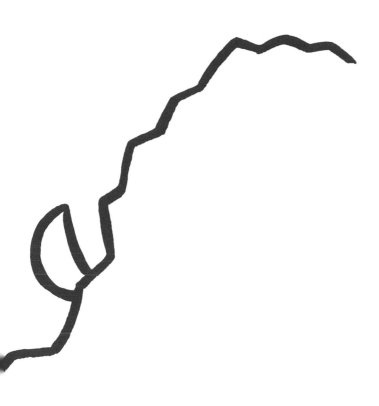

And there wasn't any other side of the
mountain. He was falling, in thin air.

But, luckily, he kept his wits and his
purple crayon.

He made a balloon and he grabbed on to it.

And he made a basket under the balloon big
enough to stand in.

He had a fine view from the balloon but he
couldn't see his window. He couldn't even
see a house.

So he made a house, with windows.

And he landed the balloon on the grass in
the front yard.

None of the windows was his window.

He tried to think where his window ought
to be.

He made some more windows.

He made a big building full of windows.

He made lots of buildings full of windows.

He made a whole city full of windows.

But none of the windows was his window.

He couldn't think where it might be.

He decided to ask a policeman.

The policeman pointed the way Harold was
going anyway. But Harold thanked him.

And he walked along with the moon,
wishing he was in his room and in bed.

Then, suddenly, Harold remembered.

He remembered where his bedroom window
was, when there was a moon.

It was always right around the moon.

And then Harold made his bed.

He got in it and he drew up the covers.

The purple crayon dropped on the floor.

And Harold dropped off to sleep.

to the
enchanted
garden

Harold's Fairy Tale

One evening Harold got out of bed, took his purple crayon and the moon along, and went for a walk in an enchanted garden.

Nothing grew in it. If he hadn't known it
was an enchanted garden, Harold scarcely
would have called it a garden at all.

To find out what the trouble was, Harold

decided to ask the king.

Kings live in large castles. Harold had to
make sure the castle was big enough to be
the king's.

He didn't want to waste time talking to
any princes or earls, or dukes.

This was a king's castle all right. It had
tall towers and a big draw-gate to keep out
people the king didn't want to see.

But when the draw-gate was drawn closed

it kept Harold out too.

Harold shouted for the king to come down
and let him in. But the gate didn't open.

He walked along the edge of the enchanted
garden beside the smooth wall of the castle
—until he thought of his purple crayon.

A person smaller than a very small mouse

would be able to get in.

Without even bending, he walked into a
very small mousehole.

He walked through the mousehole into

the castle. He invited the mouse in too,

but the mouse preferred to stay outside.

As he gazed around inside the big castle

Harold felt very tiny.

And a king might not pay much attention
to anybody who was smaller than a mouse.
So Harold used his purple crayon again.

He made sure he was as tall as four and
a half steps of stairs, his usual height.

Then he climbed up the stairs, looking
for the king.

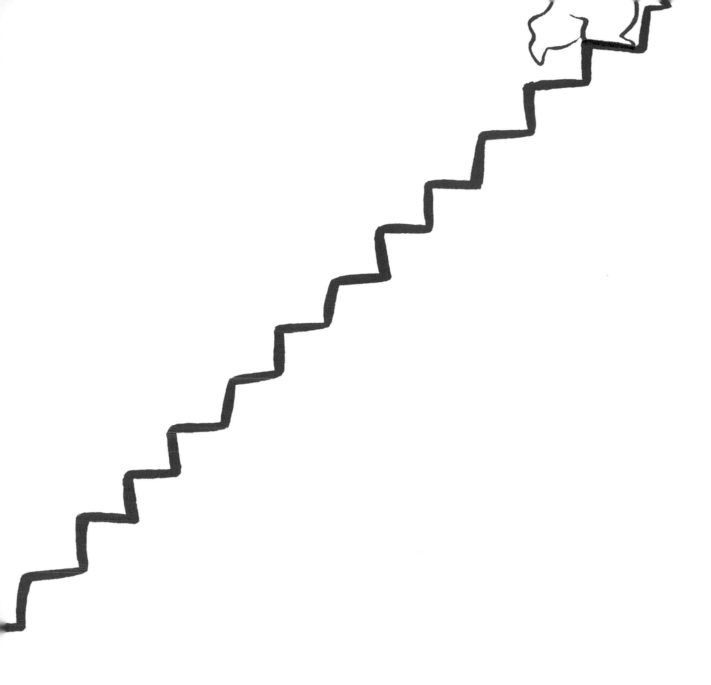

He went up and up and up, until he got so
tired he couldn't climb another step.

Luckily there were no more steps. He had
reached the top.

He still couldn't find the king. But he
remembered kings sat on thrones.

The king's throne looked very comfortable.
Harold thought the king wouldn't mind if
he rested a few minutes.

He sat on the throne, wondering what it
was like to be a king and wear a crown.

He tried it, with the king's crown.

It was all right for a while. But the

crown began to feel heavy.

So Harold put it on the king's head.

As he thanked the king for the loan of
the crown, he noticed the king looked
sad—no doubt because of the garden.

He asked the king if the trouble was due
to a witch or a giant. The king couldn't
say which. He looked sad and helpless.

Evidently the giant or witch—if the king

couldn't tell which it was—was invisible.

But Harold told the king not to worry.

He set off to find the invisible witch or
giant, brandishing his purple crayon. And
—accidently—it made a hole in the wall.

The accident embarrassed Harold. But
the hole was the handiest way out of the
castle and he climbed through it.

When he looked down from the other side
of the hole, he realized he had forgotten
how high up he was.

He needed something tall to climb down on, something as tall as a steeple.

To fill the hole in the castle, Harold put
a handsome and useful clock in it. He was
surprised to see how late it was.

He slid down the steeple, to find the
invisible witch or giant right away.

It wasn't a steeple. It was a pointed hat.

It was a GIANT WITCH.

The purple crayon made it plain—it was
an invisible giant witch. Well, no wonder
nothing grew in the enchanted garden.

How could anything grow, Harold said
to himself, with a giant witch tramping
around with big feet.

Now that he saw what the trouble was, all
Harold had to do was drive the witch out
of the enchanted garden.

Mosquitoes. Mosquitoes, Harold knew, will
drive anybody out of a garden.

The mosquitoes drove out the witch. They

also were driving Harold out of the garden.

He had to make smoke to get rid of the
mosquitoes.

And he had once heard somebody say that where there's smoke there must be fire.

To put out the fire, he first thought of
fire engines. But he decided to make it
rain. Rain was easier.

The rain soaked everything—Harold too.

But, he said, it's good for the flowers.

He was right. Soon there were flowers.

Beautiful flowers popped up all over the
enchanted garden, more than Harold was
able to count, all in gorgeous bloom.

Harold thought how delighted and happy
the king would be when he looked out
from the castle in the morning.

And then, amazingly, the last flower
turned out to be not a flower at all—
but a lovely fairy.

She held out her magic wand as fairies
always do when they're giving somebody
wishes that will come true.

Harold couldn't think of a thing to wish for. But, to be polite, he took one wish and told the fairy he'd use it later.

Besides, Harold thought, as he started on his long walk home, a wish might come in handy sometime.

After all the excitement he suddenly felt
tired. And he stopped to rest awhile.

He sat on a small rug because the ground
was still somewhat damp from the rain.
And he wished—

He wished the rug was a flying carpet.

At once Harold felt it rise in the air.

It flew fast and high.

But when it went so fast it left the moon
behind, Harold realized he didn't know how
to stop the carpet, or even slow it down.

He wished he'd taken two wishes from the
fairy, so he could wish the flying carpet
would land.

But he did have his purple crayon.

He landed the flying carpet in his living
room, right behind the high-backed chair
his mother sat in, knitting.

And he asked her to read him a story

before he went back to bed.

A B C
E F G H I J K
L M N O P Q
R S T U V W
X Y Z _____

HAROLD'S
ABC

A B C
E F G H I J K
L M N O P Q
R S T U V W
X Y Z _____

Harold decided one evening to take a trip
through the alphabet, from **A** to **Z**.

D

To go on any kind of trip he had to leave
home. He started with A for Attic.

And he left his yard, taking his purple
crayon and the moon along.

To get very far he was going to need a lot of words. B is for Books.

He could find plenty of words in a pile of
big books. He was ready for anything.

Harold was always ready for something to eat. And C is for Cake.

He took a large cut of cake and ate it as
he continued on his way.

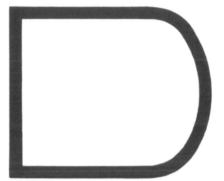

The cake made him thirsty, and he wanted
a drink.   Luckily D is for Drink.

He drank right out of the dipper. He was
eager to get on with his excursion.

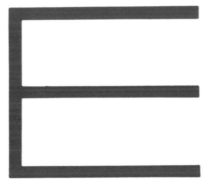

He visited an enormous edifice, the tallest
building in the world.

It went up and up and up, floor after floor,
etcetera, etcetera. E is for Etcetera.

Elevators take people up and down in big buildings, but Harold didn't like them.

They made his stomach feel funny. He went
up, over a hundred stories, in his own way.

At the very top Harold was surprised to
see something higher than he was.

It was only the next letter of the alphabet,
flying from the roof. F is for Flag.

Now he had to get down. G is for Giant.
One happened to be passing by.

Giants generally aren't so genial. But this
one grinned when Harold landed on him.

Harold explained he was in a hurry. The
giant gently set him on the ground.

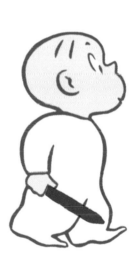

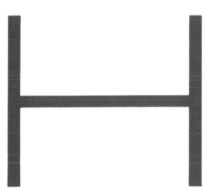

He hastened along. H is for Horse. One
way to go fast is on horseback.

Unfortunately the horse didn't turn out to look much like a real horse.

It made a rather good hobby horse, but a hobby horse doesn't go anywhere.

Harold had to think of some other way to speed his trip. I is for Idea.

He went to work on the next letter with
his purple crayon. J is for Jet.

In a jiffy he had a speedy little jet plane
ready to take off.

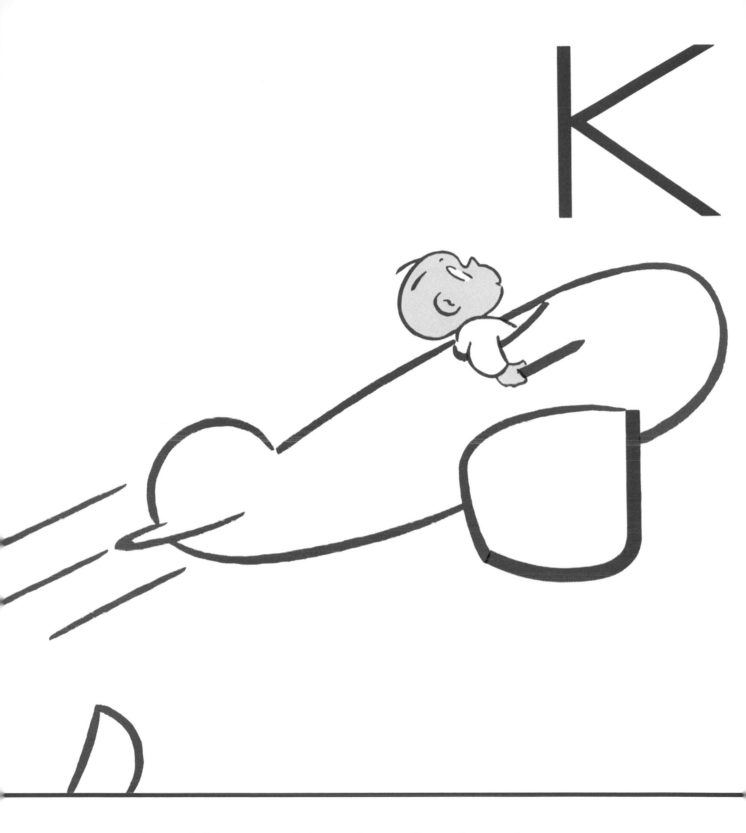

Harold hopped into it and rocketed away.
It overtook the next letter in no time.

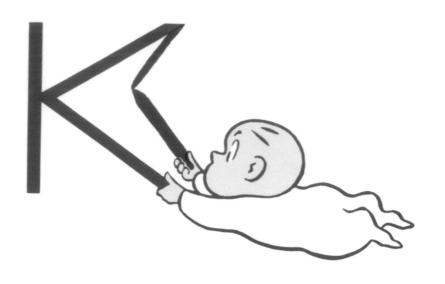

Harold jumped out and grabbed on,
thinking hard of a word for it.

K is for Kite, flying on a string.   Harold
began to climb down the string.

L

Suddenly a quicker way of getting down
struck Harold.

L is for Lightning. Harold held tight to
the purple crayon, going like a streak.

He landed on a pair of tall peaks, high and
lonely.   M is for Mountain.

He looked for somebody to ask where these
mountains were.   N is for Nobody.

Off in the sky he saw an orbiting object.
It looked like a strange planet.

O is for Ours. Our earth! The mountains
were on the rim of the moon.

He looked over the edge, at the side of
the moon he had never seen.

Down below him was the next letter of the
alphabet. Taking aim, he jumped.

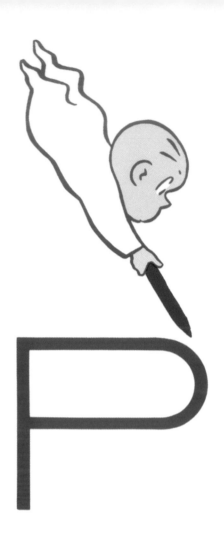

P is for Parachute, he said as he plunged
to a plain on the far side of the moon.

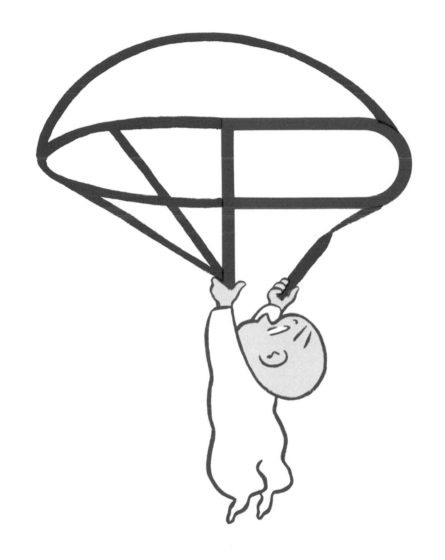

And suddenly he wondered how he could
get back over the ridge of mountains.

He would have to ask the man in the moon,
or the king, or whoever was in charge.

Q is for Queen. She was Urania, queen of
the sky, she told Harold, who bowed.

Only King Uranus could help Harold get home, she said, but the king was away.

Far away, the queen said, across land and
sea. Harold decided to ride there.

R is for Rhinoceros, roaming both land and water. But it was a slow rough ride.

S

And when Harold reached the sea, and the
next letter, he had a better idea.

S is for Sea Serpent.   Harold sailed across
the moon ocean at a smooth swift speed.

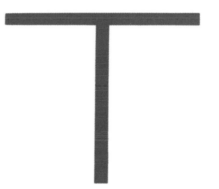

He landed far away, looking for the king of the sky who was supposed to be there.

T is for Telescope.   He set it up on a tripod.
All he saw through it was another letter.

The queen had mentioned the king's name.
Harold remembered it. U is for Uranus.

He drew the king's attention and asked how
to get back across the moon mountains.

King Uranus in his ermine robe stood silent
and majestic, considering the question.

Then, with a kingly gesture, he waved Harold forward and onward.

Harold trudged along toward another letter,
away off in the distance.

It was V for Valley.   He could go through it
to the side of the moon near the earth.

Four more letters and he would be through
the whole alphabet.

But the biggest letter of all barred his way.
He tried to think of a word for it, quickly.

W is for Witch, wicked and waiting. And it looked as if he would never get through.

Harold nearly gave up. But then he saw the
next letter, right near by.

X is for Xxxing-Out.   Harold had had to X
things out before, lots of times.

It worked this time too. Witches are very
susceptible to such treatment.

He had made so many marks it was hard to
get through them, but Harold managed.

Magically he found himself in a familiar
garden, with the moon high in the sky.

D

E

Y is for Yard, his own yard.   He was home!
And there was one letter left.

In his bedroom, as he dozed off, he made up
a word.   Z is for Zzzl, or little snore.

Afterword

Crockett Johnson and the Purple Crayon

by Philip Nel

Crockett Johnson never had much money growing up in Queens, New York, but he had his imagination. As soon as he could hold a crayon, he started drawing. Once Crockett learned his letters, he started writing stories, too. When he was fourteen, his school magazine began publishing his cartoons. This is the first one.

D. J. Leisk, "An Off Day," Newtown High School Lantern, March 1921.

Why is this signed "D. J. Leisk" and not "Crockett Johnson"? Although the creator of *Harold and the Purple Crayon* was born David Johnson Leisk (pronounced *Lisk*), there were many other boys named David in the neighborhood, so he borrowed "Crockett" from a comic strip about frontiersman Davy Crockett. In high school, he still signed his cartoons with his real first and middle initials and his real last name. Later, he decided that "Leisk" was too difficult to pronounce. So he added his childhood nickname to his middle name and came up with Crockett Johnson.

Crockett Johnson at age seventeen.

GOING TO WORK

At seventeen, Johnson went to Cooper Union, where he studied art, typography, and drawing. But he almost did not become an artist at all.

When Johnson was eighteen, his father died, and he had to go to work. He gave up his study of art. For the next ten years, there were no new cartoons by Crockett Johnson—or D. J. Leisk.

He got work as a magazine art editor, which was good training for someone who would later create picture books. Art editors decide what each page looks like: How many pictures? What size should each picture be?

After the October 1929 stock market crash, Johnson began to draw what he saw happening around him. It was the Depression. The richest Americans were still living well, but everyone else was not. In 1934, he started publishing his cartoons in *New Masses*, a weekly Communist magazine. He hoped his cartoons might lead people to create a country where everyone (and not just the rich) had a chance of a good job, a nice home, and enough to eat.

FALLING IN LOVE

In 1939, at a party in New York, Crockett Johnson met a writer named Ruth Krauss. She was slim and small at five feet, four inches tall. He was nearly six feet tall. She was outgoing and full of energy. He was quiet and almost shy. Both had already been married once. By the end of that party, they knew that they would be together. As Krauss liked to say, "We met and that was it!"

Crockett Johnson, Ruth Krauss, and their dogs, Sean and Gonsel, in Darien, Connecticut, 1944. The following year, they moved to Rowayton, Connecticut, where they lived until 1972.

FINDING A FAIRY GODFATHER

Soon they would marry and become famous writers of children's picture books. But first, Johnson became the creator of the comic strip *Barnaby*. In the 1940s, comic strip creators were as well known as actors or athletes are today. In the first *Barnaby* strip, a five-year-old boy named Barnaby wishes for a fairy godmother. Instead, he gets Mr. O'Malley, a fairy godfather who uses a cigar for a magic wand and only sometimes gets his magic to work.

Crockett Johnson poses with the artwork for the cover of his book Barnaby (1943).

The grown-ups think Barnaby has imagined his fairy godfather, but child characters and readers know that O'Malley exists. Explaining how he reached young readers, Crockett Johnson said, "When it comes to knowing about children, it's a terribly old thing to say, but everyone was once a child himself."

JOHNSON WRITES FOR CHILDREN

While writing *Barnaby*, Johnson started illustrating children's books. His first picture book was Ruth Krauss's *The Carrot Seed*, published in 1945. It is the story of a little boy who knows his carrot will come up, even though everyone says it won't. He is right. The book became a bestseller and a classic. It was the first big success for both Johnson and Krauss in children's books.

Original edition of The Carrot Seed.

197

THE COLOR OF ADVENTURE

Where did the idea for *Harold and the Purple Crayon* come from? Crockett Johnson never answered that question. In December 1955, a reporter asked why Harold's crayon was purple. Johnson simply replied, "Purple is the color of adventure." Is this a serious answer? I don't know.

I do know that Harold was inspired by three different children.

Crockett Johnson's cover drawing of Harold, for Harold and the Purple Crayon.

THE REAL HAROLDS

One child who inspired Harold is young Crockett Johnson himself. Johnson and Harold both began drawing as young children. Both are bald artists who like to work at night. Both know that quick thinking and creativity can solve problems.

David Johnson Leisk and his mother, Mary, in an undated photo

Another child behind Harold was Nina Wallace. She was the only child of close friends of Johnson and Krauss. They lived right across the street, and Nina's mother, Phyllis Rowand, illustrated three of Krauss's picture books. In September 1954, after a car accident killed Nina's father, Johnson became a father figure to

Nina Wallace, c. 1949.

198

eight-year-old Nina. She became the daughter that he and Krauss never had. In his home office, Johnson built a Nina-sized chair and desk. While she sat at her small desk drawing pictures, he sat at his larger one, writing a book about a child who draws pictures. He finished *Harold and the Purple Crayon* in November 1954—the same month that Nina turned nine.

The third child loaned Harold his name. In 1953, Johnson's sister, Else Frank, and her husband, Leonard Frank, adopted a boy. They named him Harold for the lawyer who helped with the adoption, and David for Else's father and brother. Johnson borrowed his character's name from his nearly two-year-old nephew, Harold David Frank.

Harold Frank, c. 1955

DRAWING A WORLD

The Harold books' main idea—of living in a world that you're also drawing—is how some children feel when they draw. They feel as if the rest of the world has dropped away, leaving just them, their crayons, and the page. Johnson might have been remembering his own childhood experience of drawing.

Or he might have been thinking of others who live in the art they are making. Johnson was not the first to come up with a character who creates his own world. But he was the first to build a children's picture book on this idea. And when you're the first, people don't always understand what you're doing.

Artist Crockett Johnson as drawn by Harold.

Crockett Johnson as drawn by Harold, 1958.

HAROLD ALMOST NEVER HAPPENED

When Johnson's illustrated rough draft of *Harold and the Purple Crayon* arrived on her desk, Ursula Nordstrom—his editor at Harper & Brothers—was puzzled. "I don't know what to say about it. It doesn't seem to be a good children's book to me, but I'm often wrong." She asked Harper reader Ann Powers to take a look. At first, Ann didn't know what to say either. But she soon changed her mind, saying, "The more I look at the book, the more I like it."

Nordstrom changed her mind, too, and apologized: "I think it is going to make a darling book, and I certainly was wrong at first."

11/22/54

Dear Dave:

The dummy of HAROLD AND THE PURPLE CRAYON came this morning, and I've just read it. I don't know what to say about it. It doesn't seem to be a good children's book to me but I'm often wrong - and this post-Children's Book Week Monday finds me dead in the head. I'd probably pass up TOM SAWYER today. Let me keep the dummy a few days, will you? I want Ann Powers to read it. She's young and fresh (not sassy, you understand) and less tired than I am. And I'd like to read it again myself when I'm a little more caught up.

I found myself asking such dumb questions - like where did he draw the moon and the path and the tree? And then when I got far enough to realize he was dreaming, OF COURSE, I was puzzled by the moon in the last picture. You can see from this heavy-handed comment that I didn't read the story with much imagination.

I hate to send you this sort of a nothing letter. But I wanted to send you some sort of word and this is the best I can do today. We'll keep the dummy a little longer and I'll write you again soon, or call you up.

Yours,

Ursula

Crockett Johnson

I see some charm in this book, and I think it holds one's engrossed attention from beginning to end, and even bears rereadings. I don't think it is anything sensational, but it is a little different. What makes me think children would like it is that I know how they enjoy those animated advertising cartoons on TV, where the pictures are drawn right before your eyes, in line, as if with a pencil. Also, that Danny Dee story program uses this technique and apparently it is very successful. This book resembles the animated cartoon very closely; in this case, the character in the story does the drawing, which is better in a book, since the author does not have to be evident, and the story is given a central point and continuous movement. The parts I like best, and think children would enjoy, are: the dragon, falling into the sea, the sailboat, the picnic with the two animals to finish up, the climbing u and falling off the mountain, the balloon, the building the policeman, the bed. As you point out, there is a question as to whether the moon should appear in the la picture or not. I suppose it could have come out by that time; otherwise it could be left as the only remaining part of the dream. The parts I am not too sure of are:

(over)

---

the pathway at the beginning (too strange?); the forest which is not a forest (too arch?); the apples would be tasty when red (pointless? unnecessary?); came up thinking fast (pun?); 1st picture drawing sail--he's not drawing it the way it is going to finally be; house & buildings-- why should he look for his room in both a small house and a large apt. building--he knows the difference and can't be confused; policeman pointing (arch?).

Otherwise, the more I look at the book, the more I like it. I'm not crazy for CJ's bald kewpie boy; I think he should be given some hair, regardless of CJ's 'famous' style. The book is different and appealing; whether it is worthy of a $2.00 format is another question. I wouldn't want to pay over $1.00 for it, probably less; but then I feel that way about at least 3/4 of all children's books (likewise with adult books, priced in proportion). Libraries will probably not get excited over the book because it will most likely look like cartoon work to them, particularly if they have to decide to buy without actually seeing the book. And then, this is undoubtedly one of those books which are indescribable in copy.

Above: The original letter from Ursula to Crockett concerning Harold and the Purple Crayon *and a note to Ursula from Ann Powers, who liked* Harold *and helped her see his appeal.*

HAROLD IS A HIT

Crockett Johnson, poster for Spring 1958 Children's Book Festival, sponsored by the Herald Tribune.

Less than a month after *Harold*'s fall 1955 publication, the book had sold ten thousand copies. Nordstrom wrote to Johnson: "I know you don't want to do *Harold and His Green Crayon* or *Harold and His Orange Crayon*, but I honestly think further adventures of Harold would sell and not be a cheap idea either."

By year's end, Johnson finished a draft of *Harold's Fairy Tale*. Harold's crayon would remain purple for all seven of his adventures.

The *New York Times* predicted that Harold would "probably start youngsters off on odysseys of their own." It did. Former US Poet Laureate Rita Dove says *Harold* was her first favorite book because "it showed me the possibility of traveling along the line of one's imagination." Picture book creator Chris Van Allsburg says *Harold* is the childhood book he remembers best because of its "theme, which has to do with the ability to create things with your imagination."

Thanks to the success of *Harold and the Purple Crayon*, children's books became Johnson's job for the next several years. Between 1954 and 1967, he created nineteen picture books, co-created one (with Krauss), and illustrated six others (including two by Krauss). The books have been translated into nineteen languages around the world.

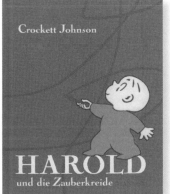

Harold in Chinese, Hebrew, and German.

LIFE AFTER HAROLD

Then Johnson stopped making picture books. Between 1965 and 1975, he painted over one hundred pictures inspired by mathematical theorems. He even published two original theorems of his own. By early July of 1975, Johnson—a lifelong smoker—lay in his hospital bed, dying of lung cancer. Seeing the worried look on Johnson's face, his friend Gil Rose asked, "What would Harold do?" Johnson began thinking about his illness from Harold's point of view. He relaxed.

Since Harold always kept "his wits and his purple crayon," let us imagine him drawing a boat, and Johnson stepping on board. With Harold at the helm and a purple-edged moon lighting their way, the small boy and his creator set sail, charting a course on the vast canvas of the imagination.

Johnson died a few days later. He was sixty-eight.

But Harold lives on, inspiring us to keep drawing and dreaming.

Crockett Johnson and his painting, Heptagon from Seven Sides, *1972.*